CRABTREE SCHOOL

Best Friends for Never

Lauren Pearson

Illustrated by Becka Moor

SCHOLASTIC

For all the best friends: Mary Katherine and Kelly and Jenny and Anne and Ashley and Lisa and Jill and Erin and Carrie and Christy and Jacqueline and Sarah and Uma and Shirit and Zoe and Helen and Pri. And especially for Susan Henry Quick, my very own bestest of best friends forever

Chapter

Bubble Bubble, Here Comes Trouble

In a shady back garden somewhere on the edge of Crabtree Lane, two heads bent over a cauldron. Water from the pond in Crabtree Park simmered inside the huge pot, mixed with autumn leaves and shiny red crab apples. A tiny boat bobbed on the surface of this magical soup, and two necklaces – two halves of one heart – lay gently on a lacy pillow on the small ship's deck.

"Now for your bit," said Ava, brushing her wispy blonde hair back from her face and drying her hands on her jeans.

Zoe stepped forward, her wellies squelching in the mud of the soggy flower bed. She opened her rucksack.

"Here I give you my favourite things," she said in her most serious voice. "Here is the maths test I got full marks on." Taking care not to sink the boat, Zoe dropped the test paper into the cauldron and stirred it round until it sank to the bottom.

"And here is a star sticker from the ceiling of my bedroom, and a peacock feather I found at the zoo. Here is the ticket from when we went to see *Frozen*." She stirred the mixture once again.

"My turn," said Ava, as a fine mist crept over the garden. She stepped forward. "By all the mystical magical powers in the universe, I add this bit of hair from my hairbrush—"

"Ewww!" Zoe shrieked and they both giggled.

Ava continued solemnly. "Here is the last page of *Pippi Longstocking*, my most favourite book in the entire world." Another sheet of paper vanished into the cauldron.

"And finally, here is my ticket from *Frozen*," finished Ava. "Now we must recite the sacred poem."

The two girls joined hands and began the chant:

"Eeeny, meeny, miney, mo,
No matter where we one day go,
Eeny, meeny, miney, mee,
The best of friends we'll always be."

The garden grew deathly silent. All those present – the dolls seated round the cauldron, the garden gnome, Ava's cat and even the birds – were perfectly still, watching and waiting. Everything had to be just right.

Finally, at long last, Zoe was sure that she could see the two necklaces on the boat begin to glow: the spell was working!

"Ava, Zoe, pizza time!" Ava's mum shouted from the kitchen door. She stepped outside. "Look at you two, you are covered in mud! And why on earth are you mucking about with that old paddling pool? The water is filthy!"

Zoe and Ava rescued their necklaces just as the spell faded.

"Remember," said Zoe, "we must never take these off." She held up her half of the friendship heart. It read:

"Never, for as long as we both shall live and happily ever after and all of those things," agreed Ava. Her half read:

As they made their way towards the warm light of the kitchen, neither Zoe nor Ava noticed the slimy green frog that jumped out of the cauldron. If they had, they might have seen it as a bad omen. Best friend spells are the most difficult of all spells to cast properly, and even one extra ingredient can spoil the whole lot.

"But, Mummy," cried Zoe that evening at bath time, "I CAN'T take my necklace off. I promised to wear it forever and ever and as long as—"

"I'm sure Ava will understand that you need to have a bath and you don't want your necklace to get ruined," said Zoe's mum. "Ava will have to take hers off too, for her bath. Now get going, you're a muddy mess."

There was no arguing with Zoe's mum, especially when it was nearly bedtime. Very carefully, Zoe put her half of the heart on a towel by the side of the tub and climbed into the bubbles.

It would probably be OK, Zoe decided. She and Ava loved a bit of magic, but even without it they were already the best of friends there could ever be. At school, Zoe and Ava were always together. They sat next to each other at the lunch table and they played together at break time. They were always partners in PE, and they stood in every queue side-by-side. Last spring, they had become the youngest girls ever in the history of their school to win the wheelbarrow race during Sports Day. That had made them sort of famous. Everyone at Crabtree School for Girls knew that Ava and Zoe were best friends.

When they weren't at school, Zoe and Ava had play dates all the time, even sleepovers. They built forts out of sofa cushions. They dressed up in Ava's mummy's old clothes and borrowed Zoe's daddy's telescope to look at the stars. Last summer, they'd seen each other every day for thirteen days in a row. By the thirteenth day, they were finishing each other's sentences in a made-up language that only the two of them could understand.

"Mofnwoh," Zoe would say. "Zmmbob—"

"Zmmbob maywee gllloople," Ava would agree.

Zoe knew that even without spells she and Ava would be best friends forever.

All the same, as soon as she stepped out of the bath, Zoe wasted no time putting her half of the Best Friends heart safely back around her neck.

Chapter

The Most Horrible Maths
Lesson in the World

Zoe liked numbers. Ava always said that Zoe wanted to marry numbers. If she *were* going to marry a number, Zoe would choose seven. Seven was her favourite number and also her age.

Because of this love of numbers, Zoe was always counting things. On the first day of Year Three at Crabtree School for Girls, Zoe had counted the desks in their new classroom. There were three rows of desks, and there were seven desks in each row.

The sum could look like this:

7 desks + 7 desks + 7 desks = 21 desks

There were twenty-one girls in their class, so Zoe had known right from the beginning of Year Three that each girl would have her very own desk. This was different from Year Two, when they had sat at four big tables. Year Three was much more grown-up.

One thing numbers *couldn't* tell you about the desks in Year Three was that on the first day of school, you got to choose your own place. You could sit wherever you wanted, even next to your best friend. By the time they had cast the magic friendship spell, Ava and Zoe had been sitting next to each other in the Year Three classroom for seventeen days.

That morning, on the eighteenth day, Zoe had come racing into Year Three to tell Ava about the fox she'd seen on the way to school, the fox that was walking straight down the middle of the road as if it were going to the bus stop. But Ava wasn't in her seat in the second row near the window, because something terrible had happened.

Year Three was all in a jumble. There was one row of seven desks at the back. Then there was another row of six desks, then one of five and then one final row of four desks in the front by the teacher.

Now the sum looked like this:

7 desks + 6 desks + 5 desks + 4 desks = 22 desks

There were twenty-two desks in the Year Three classroom, which meant that there was one more desk today than there had been last week.

Zoe hardly had time to think about this, because her own desk had been moved as well. She could tell from the names written on the tops that her desk was an *entire row* away from Ava's desk and across the whole room. She was miles away from her best friend.

This did not make sense. It did not add up.

Zoe saw that Ava was unhappy too, and not just because she and Zoe were so far apart. Ava was no longer near a window. Zoe knew that Ava liked to stare out at the park and the clouds. She liked to daydream nearly all the time, and that would be a lot harder from her new seat in the middle of Year Three. Zoe felt sorry for her best friend.

Zoe = miserable, Ava = miserable, and for what? None of this added up.

Zoe and Ava were not the only ones having a disaster. Their friend Lottie had also lost her seat near the window. Now Lottie was in a middle row towards the front. Lottie was the nosiest girl at Crabtree School for Girls. She liked to know everything about everyone. From her new place, Lottie couldn't see out of the window to watch people coming and going with her huge brown eyes. She couldn't see the classroom door or the hallway properly either, and she would miss out on everything that was going on behind her. Worst of all, now Lottie was close to the teacher's desk, which meant that Miss Moody might catch her spying, or writing in her purple notebook.

Zoe = miserable, Ava = miserable, Lottie = miserable.

Why would Miss Moody do this to them? Why would she let them choose their seats for the beginning of Year Three and then go and ruin everything?

Their friend Isabel was luckier. Isabel was the best-behaved, most helpful, kindest girl in their class, and she always sat in the front row. This morning was like every other morning for Isabel; she was right there in her same seat, sitting with her hands folded, her desk tidy, waiting for school to begin. Her plaits seemed especially straight and even her freckles looked organized. Plus, now Isabel was even closer to Lottie, who was *her* best friend.

The four of them, Isabel, Lottie, Ava and Zoe, stuck together like chocolate buttons on a warm day. They were friends and they always had been, ever since Reception. Ava and Zoe were *the bestest of best* friends, and Lottie and Isabel were *the bestest of best* friends, but it could safely be said that all four of them were very, very good friends.

2 bestest friends + 2 bestest friends = 4 very, very good friends.

It was perfect maths, really, because it all came out evenly.

Except, right then, Zoe secretly wanted to pinch Isabel a little bit. Because it really wasn't fair that she got to stay in her same seat while everyone else moved. *Maybe*, Zoe thought hopefully, *Isabel would be sat next to someone*

that she didn't like. That would even things out.

The trouble with that was that their Year Three class was really quite special. Everyone at Crabtree School said so. They all got on and, for the most part, everybody liked everybody else. *Still,* Zoe thought, looking around Year Three, *there had to be someone that Isabel might not want to sit next to.* Margot talked a lot, even when she wasn't supposed to, and Louisa never sat still. Maybe Isabel, who was very keen on following the rules, would be sat next to a chatterbox or a wiggler. Then Isabel would be cross, and that would make it fair.

But the name on the desk next to Isabel did not say Margot. It did not say Louisa. It said Rani.

This was very strange because there was no one in the class of twenty-one girls called Rani.

But as you know:

7 desks + 6 desks + 5 desks + 4 desks = 22 desks.

Not twenty-one.

Chapter

Apple Crumble, Fairy Lights and a Smiley Cat

"Take your seats, girls," said Miss Moody cheerfully. Despite her name – Miss Moody is a dreadful name for a teacher – Miss Moody was not at all moody. In fact, she was perfectly cheery. Zoe thought she should have been called Miss Good-Moody. But today she must have gone bonkers. What was she thinking, moving everyone's seats?

Because she didn't know what else to do, Zoe sat down in her horrible new place and got ready for the lesson to begin. She smoothed down her curly brown hair and straightened the six clips she always wore to keep it tidy, three on each side of her head. She took out her Monday pencil and made sure that it was nice and sharp. Zoe had a different pencil for every day of the week. Monday's pencil was pink, which happened to be Ava's favourite colour. Zoe looked sadly down at her necklace. Even if Miss Moody had forgotten that best friends should sit together, surely the Best Friend spell should be working to keep her and Ava close?

Zoe couldn't even *see* Ava at that moment, she was so far away. In front of Zoe, Lottie was writing furiously in her notebook, while at the same time wiggling her hand in the air for Miss Moody's attention. The new desk arrangement and the mysterious name tag were probably driving Lottie mad; spies like Lottie didn't like surprises. But before Lottie could demand an explanation from Miss Moody, the class was interrupted by a visit from the headmistress of

Crabtree School for Girls.

Mrs Peabody was a headmistress of legendary kindness. Not only did she know the name of every girl at Crabtree School, she knew their favourite colours and their baby brothers' names and what they liked on their pizzas. Mrs Peabody gave out lots of hugs, and if you happened to be passing by her office at the right time of day, she'd offer you hot chocolate and a biscuit. Sometimes two biscuits. The headmistress wore bright summery colours even in darkest winter. She had poufy grey hair that was swirled high on her head in two big bubbles; Zoe thought it looked like a number eight. Mrs Peabody's shoes made lovely tippety-tappety music when she walked, and she smelled of sweet perfume and also of biscuits. She was one of the best things about Crabtree School – which was saying a lot, because Crabtree School was full of wonderful things.

Mrs Peabody only had one weakness that anyone could see, and it may have been just the thing that made her so kind: Mrs Peabody hated to see a child cry. It drove her bananas. Her skin would go red, her eyes would pop out and her hair would stand straight up. Then her teeth would chatter and she'd talk complete nonsense. Zoe had seen it happen many times.

So it was very worrying that standing next to Mrs Peabody was a girl with big dark eyes, soft brown skin and huge tears rolling down her cheeks.

"Girls," said Mrs Peabody, "I am delighted to introduce you to Miss Rani Anand. Rani will be joining you in Year Three. Isn't that exciting?"

Zoe noticed that although Mrs Peabody was patting Rani reassuringly on the back, the headmistress couldn't bring herself to actually *look* at the new girl. Already Rani's tears were causing little puffs of smoke to come out of

Mrs Peabody's nose and ears.

Miss Moody came to the rescue. "That's wonderful news, Mrs Peabody," she said. "Rani, welcome to Year Three! How delightful to have you here!"

Rani did not look delighted. She looked sad and most of all scared. Zoe studied her carefully. Rani had on pink sparkly nail polish, and her school shoes were the kind that could be decorated with bows and jewels.

Miss Moody showed Rani her desk next to Isabel's.

"Isabel," said Miss Moody kindly. "Please will you look after Rani today? Will you show her around during break time? Give her a little tour of our school?"

Isabel couldn't have looked happier, which Zoe thought was strange because this meant Isabel would miss playing at break time. Their daily game of Mummies and Babies in the

Crabtree School tree house would be ruined, because Isabel was always the mummy and now they wouldn't have one.

Lottie's hand shot up in the air again.

"Please may I help too, Miss Moody? I can tell Rani loads about Crabtree School."

Miss Moody had to agree that no one had more information about Crabtree School than Lottie. Everything you ever wanted to know (and more) was right there in her purple notebook.

So Lottie was allowed to help, and now break time Mummies and Babies would be missing the daddy too.

The version of Mummies and Babies that Zoe, Ava, Lottie and Isabel played wasn't the kind that little children play; it was much more complicated than that. They went on camping trips under the slide and started fires by rubbing sticks together. (They hadn't actually started a real fire yet, but it was only a matter of time.) They had beach holidays in the sandpit and they went to see the doctor next to the climbing frame to sort out bouts of chickenpox made with red pen. Zoe, Ava, Lottie and Isabel were expert pretenders. Mostly Isabel was Mum, Lottie was Dad, and Zoe was the baby, because she had a baby brother and was therefore an expert on babies. Ava was usually some sort of animal or lifeguard or doctor. Now today all they'd have was a baby and probably a kitten, which really wasn't a family at all. It would be just a lot of crying and mewing.

Zoe scowled. She watched Rani's back as Crabtree's newest student put her things into her desk. Probably Rani was a perfectly nice girl (she had lots of sharp sparkly pencils, that was for sure) but why did everyone have to use break time to show her around the school? At least Zoe would still have Ava. Maybe Ava would agree to be a big sister, and they could pretend the mummy and daddy had been kidnapped by pirates.

Then a dreamy voice called out, "Please may I help too, Miss Moody?"

Zoe knew who that was even before she twisted round to look.

"Of course you can, Ava," said Miss Moody, who was pleased that everyone was so eager to help Rani settle in, and also pleased that Ava had been paying attention and not daydreaming.

Morning break time was now well and truly ruined. Zoe couldn't very well sit in the Crabtree tree house crying and goo-goo gaa-gaa-ing all by herself. She sighed and put her hand up. Rani would have four tour guides.

Crabtree School was quite simply the best primary school in all of Great Britain. Everyone for miles around knew this to be true, and Zoe for one couldn't understand why Rani would be anything but excited to be joining Crabtree's Year Three class. But Rani still looked sad when it was time for morning break. She also looked not at all sorry to have ruined a perfectly good game of Mummies and Babies. Zoe was hoping they could hurry through the tour and still have time left to play, but Isabel insisted on showing Rani every inch of Crabtree School.

First, Isabel pointed out the statue of the very first headmistress of Crabtree School, Lady Constance Hawthorne. Isabel told Rani about the legend that surrounded the little stone dog that stood at Lady Hawthorne's feet. Even though he was small and not a live dog, Baron Biscuit had guarded Crabtree School for hundreds of years. It was said that no harm could come to any Crabtree girl as long as the Baron was at his post. He had seen a lot of strange goings-on over the years.

"Don't forget to stroke him every morning," Isabel told Rani. "He brings good luck!"

"Do you like animals?" Lottie asked Rani, studying her closely. "Do you have any pets? Are you allergic to pets? Are you allergic to anything?" Lottie needed loads of information for the new RANI section in her purple notebook.

But Rani didn't want to answer Lottie's questions. She was too shy. It got very quiet and no one knew what to say.

For a minute, Zoe felt sorry for Rani. She thought about telling the story of the fox that she had seen that morning: the fox going to the bus stop. That might make Rani laugh. But before she could, a deep voice boomed, "Please don't be sad, Rani. I am Baron Biscuit, and I like to eat biscuits and sometimes I wee in the school hall. Woof, woof, woof. Bow wow-wow-wow!"

Rani jumped (they all did), and then she smiled the tiniest of smiles when she realized that the voice of Baron Biscuit was really Ava, crouched behind the statue.

"A-woofity-woof-woof," said Baron Biscuit. "Don't you like animals, Rani? Don't make me lick you!"

This time Rani actually giggled. "I do like animals, but I don't have any pets," she told Lottie. "I have four brothers and Mum says that's enough wild things in the house. I wish I had a dog more than anything."

Lottie jotted this down in her notebook and nodded approvingly. Wanting a dog was a plus in her book. Lottie had a dog. In dog years Pip was about a hundred and forty years old, but he was still a dog. Zoe thought he was a bit boring, but it was funny when he snored.

"Zoe hasn't any pets either," Lottie told Rani. "Ava has a cat, I have a dog and Isabel has three baby rabbits."

"Do you want to meet Lady Lovelypaws?" asked Isabel. "Crabtree School has its very own cat."

"Is Lady Lovelypaws a statue too?" asked Rani.

Lady Lovelypaws was not a statue. She was very much a real live cat. At the sound of her name, Lady Lovelypaws came bounding out of Mrs Peabody's office and ran towards the girls. She purred and rubbed against their legs and they stroked her fluffy white fur. Lady Lovelypaws could sense when a child was unhappy. She wound herself around Rani's legs as if to give her a big cuddle. She smiled up at Rani and rubbed her whiskers against Rani's socks. (Lady Lovelypaws really could smile; she was a most extraordinary cat.)

"She likes you!" said Ava, whilst Lottie recorded this fact in her notebook. "See, it will be like having your very own cat when you come to school!"

Zoe knew that it was a kind thing for Ava to say, but really Lady Lovelypaws belonged to all of them, equally. She belonged to every girl at Crabtree School. One cat divided one hundred and fifty-six ways didn't go very far, if you asked Zoe. But this was probably not a good time to mention that.

Joined by Lady Lovelypaws, they continued their tour. They showed Rani the school kitchen, where the dinner lady, Mrs Crunch, baked delicious lunches. Mrs Crunch gave Rani a taste of her special apple crumble. She gave Rani's tour guides each a taste too, which made Zoe feel a little less grumpy about missing break time.

The girls led Rani through the library, which was two whole floors tall, with ladders to reach the top shelves. Mrs Shush, the librarian, let

Rani choose a book. "Come back any time you like, dear," said Mrs Shush.

"She means it, too," said Isabel proudly. "You are allowed to go to the library to get a book any time you want, all day. Even if you are in class." Zoe could see that Rani was impressed. Finally the new girl was beginning to understand how lucky she was to be at their school.

Then they showed Rani the big school hall, which had a stage with special lights for concerts and plays. Behind it, there were props and scenery for every kind of show imaginable: there was baby Jesus's manger from the nativity, Father Christmas's workshop, a rainbow scene with a yellow brick road, a castle with turrets... Rani stared in awe at the collection of wondrous places. Mr Rockanroll, the music teacher, was playing the piano on the stage, and when he met Rani, he sang her

the school hymn.

After the last verse the girls led Rani out to the playground and showed her the giant tree house where they played their famous Mummies and Babies games. They pointed out the garden patch where the Green Thumb Club grew loads of vegetables. Rani met Colonel Crunch, who was Mrs Crunch's husband and the school groundskeeper. Colonel Crunch promised to build Rani a giant see-saw when she said that she loved them.

The girls also introduced Rani to Nurse Forehead, who was putting a plaster on a Reception girl's bleeding knee and offering her an emergency lollipop. "If you get sick at school," Isabel said helpfully, "Nurse Forehead has a special room with a bed you can rest on and a warm duvet and she reads you stories until your mum comes to get you. If your throat hurts, she gives you ice lollies." Not many schools had a nurse quite as special as Nurse Forehead.

Isabel saved the best for last. The Rainbow Room was absolutely the loveliest place in Crabtree School. When your class got golden tickets for being tidy in the lunch room or quiet in the corridors, you got to go there. The Rainbow Room twinkled with fairy lights and it had a fluffy rug with beanbag chairs to sit on. Lottie showed Rani the old-fashioned popcorn machine in the corner.

"When we watch films in here we get popcorn, like in the cinema," Zoe told Rani proudly.

"What is your favourite movie?" Lottie asked Rani, her pencil at the ready.

"It's called *Epic*," said Rani shyly. "It's about a girl who shrinks down to the size of a fairy."

"That's MY favourite movie too!" said Ava. "We have the SAME favourite movie!"

It turned out that Rani and Ava had the same favourite colour too, which was pink. Rani liked hot pink with sparkles and Ava liked regular pink. Zoe had always liked pink and purple equally, but as Rani and Ava went on and on about pink, Zoe wondered if perhaps pink ought to be her favourite colour after all. Best friends were supposed to like the same things, right?

They finished up their tour, and by the time morning break was over, Rani had a tummy full of apple crumble, lots of new friends both young and old, and a smile as big as the one on the face of the fluffy white cat following her every move. Even Rani had to agree that Crabtree School was a truly magical place. Ava told her about how earlier in the year, they'd had to *make* last year's Year Six class leave.

"They loved it so much, they wanted to stay forever and ever," Ava told Rani. "So we made things pretty horrible around here to get them out."

Rani probably couldn't imagine Crabtree School being horrible. The new girl's sad expression was long gone, and Zoe was glad. She was still cross about not being sat next to Ava any more, but now that Rani knew her way around and wasn't so scared, Lottie, Isabel, Ava and Zoe could get back to playing Mummies and Babies like they were supposed to.

Chapter

Christmas Comes Early

By the end of the afternoon, it was clear to Zoe that nothing was going to go like it was supposed to. In the lunch room after morning lessons, Ava had sat down next to Rani without saving room for Zoe. It was the first time in forever that Zoe and Ava weren't next to each other, but Ava was so caught up in telling Rani all about Crabtree School's Halloween Carnival that she forgot all about Zoe. Zoe had to sit across from them and it was difficult to hear over the clanging of cutlery and the chitter-chatter of the rest of Crabtree School.

"I would never want to dress up as anything scary like a witch," Rani was saying to Ava. "This year I am going to be a princess."

"Zoe was a witch last Halloween," Lottie told Rani.

"What's wrong with being a witch?" asked Zoe loudly.

"Nothing," said Rani. "I just don't like scary costumes."

"Me neither," said Ava.

This was a strange thing for Ava to say because last Halloween, Ava had gone as a spooky fairy, with a powdery white face and black glitter around her eyes. Zoe had thought Ava looked VERY scary, and it hadn't helped that she'd kept swooping around yelling "Boo" at everyone. It had been a properly scary Halloween costume, if you asked Zoe. She was going to remind Ava of this, but Ava and Rani were already talking about something else. They were looking down

41

at their lunches.

"Did you say that you are a veterinarian?" Zoe shouted across the table at Rani.

Ava and Rani laughed together. "No, a vegetarian!" said Rani. "I don't eat meat."

"Oh," said Zoe, looking at Rani's jacket potato. The rest of them had cottage pie. "Why not?"

"Because it's part of my religion," Rani told her. "Also, I like animals too much to eat them."

Rani's religion was called Hinduism. Isabel, Ava and Lottie asked Rani a million questions. Lottie needed a complete list of what Rani didn't eat. Ham and cheese sandwiches? No. Roast dinners? No, at least not the meat bit. Pepperoni pizza? No, at least not the pepperoni bit. Beans on toast? Yes.

Isabel wanted to know all about Hinduism, and were there any other rules to it, and by the end of lunch Ava had decided that *she* wasn't ever eating meat again.

"But we love cheeseburgers," Zoe reminded her. They always went for cheeseburgers before they went to the cinema with their mums.

"But I love cows too," Ava had said after thinking it over.

Zoe hadn't realized that Ava felt so strongly about cows. Best friends were supposed to know everything about each other, weren't they?

After lunch, Mummies and Babies was ruined all over again. Instead of playing properly, during second break everyone stood round Rani, asking her all about her old school and her old city and her old friends. Zoe couldn't understand why Lottie and Isabel and, worst of all, Ava wanted to hear about a place that could never be as perfect as Crabtree School for Girls. But try as she might, Zoe couldn't manage to drag her friends away to play. Even Lady Lovelypaws was glued to Rani's side.

If you asked Zoe, Rani was turning into a real problem.

That afternoon, they were all sitting in science class, learning about magnets. Magnets are objects that can be attracted to metal objects, and other magnets. Zoe knew all about them because they had loads on the refrigerator door at home.

Miss Moody told the class that magnets had both north and south poles. Two of the same poles would push apart from each other, and a north and a south would pull together. Then Miss Moody demonstrated this fact with two big magnets.

"And so, girls," Miss Moody concluded, "if I hold the magnets like this, they stick together. So I must have a north pole and a what, girls?"

Lots of hands went up, including Zoe's. The answer was easy. But Miss Moody did

not choose Zoe.

"Ava?" said Miss Moody. "North pole or south?"

Even though she wasn't near the window any more, Ava must have been daydreaming, because she said, "North Pole. Father Christmas lives at the North Pole."

Everyone laughed, even Ava and Miss Moody. Zoe loved her best friend even more for being so silly; they were so different and yet they stuck together so well. She and Ava were like magnets, Zoe thought to herself, like a north and a south pole. So she was delighted when Miss Moody told them about their science homework for the week.

"Girls," Miss Moody said. "As you must have guessed, our next science unit is going to be all about magnets. I want you to think of a way to show the class how magnets work, or how we use them every day."

Then Miss Moody said something that nearly made up for Year Three's new seating arrangement. "You can work on your own or with a partner on this, girls," she told her class. "You can choose whomever you want, just make sure you both contribute equally to the idea. We'll do our presentations on Friday, so you have a few days to work on this."

Zoe leaned round in her chair and beamed at Ava. She was already planning to ask her mum for a play date with Ava after school so that they could work on the magnet experiment. And she knew Ava was thinking the exact same thing.

Chapter

5

Three Is a Perfectly Lovely Number

The magnetic play date was not to be. At least, not for Zoe. When the girls came out of Crabtree School's big front doors, Ava's mum was already there to collect Ava. And not just Ava.

"I'm taking Rani as well," Ava's mummy told Miss Moody, who was at the school gates, shaking the girls' hands goodbye. "They've just moved in across the road from us and her mum is unpacking. I believe her mum rang Mrs Biro." Mrs Biro was the school secretary.

Rani lived across the road from Ava? Since

when? Thanks to Lottie's spying, the girls knew all about every family that lived on Crabtree Lane. Whose house had Rani taken? Zoe wondered.

"Can Zoe come too?" Ava asked her mum. "We need to plan our Christmas project together! It's about the North Pole!"

"Surely you have loads of time for that," said Ava's mum. "It isn't even Halloween!"

"It's not for Christmas, it's a magnet project," Zoe told her, pushing Ava gently aside. "I really need to come to your house today!"

"Zoe Eloise Ahlberg!" Without the girls noticing, Zoe's mum had arrived. "Did I just hear you invite yourself to Ava's house?"

"It's OK," said Ava's mum. "Normally I would have her, but today I've got Rani coming home with us. The Anands have just moved in and her parents are unpacking." As the mums were chatting, Ava's little brother, Johnny, had climbed to the tippy top of a crab apple tree. Ava's mum was trying to pull him down.

"Maybe another day," Zoe's mum told her as she turned to help. Johnny was hanging upside down in the tree pretending to be a bat. Both mummies were trying to untangle him from the branches. In his pram, Zoe's baby brother, Rafe, squealed with delight and pointed at Johnny. At least someone was happy.

"Besides," Zoe's mum told Ava's, "it's probably best just to have Rani. Three can be a difficult number, if you know what I mean."

Zoe for one did not know what her mum meant. What was wrong with the number three? Three was a great number. Three snowballs to make a snowman, three wishes from a genie — three was just fine, thank you.

Then out of the corner of her eye, Zoe spied Lottie and Isabel heading off down the street with Lottie's mum and her little sister.

Isabel and Lottie dragged Lottie's ancient dog, Pip, behind them. Zoe already knew they were planning to make him a magnetic collar and lead for the science project.

"But how can Rani come with you?" Zoe asked Ava's mum desperately. "She doesn't even know you. You could be a kidnapper! You aren't supposed to go off with strangers, you know," Zoe told Rani.

"ZOE! THAT IS QUITE ENOUGH!"

Zoe's mum smiled at Rani, who was now a bit nervous again and holding Ava's hand.

From her mum's tone of voice Zoe knew that she had a zero per cent chance of changing her mind and a one hundred per cent chance of getting into big trouble if she kept this up. Sadly she waved goodbye to Ava and they headed off in different directions, Ava and Rani still holding hands.

"Who am I supposed to play with then?" Zoe asked her mum after she'd finished her snack of three apple slices, three string cheeses and three cups of water. (Three really was such a nice number.)

"Play with Rafe," Mum said.

Even though he was still just a baby, Zoe played with Rafe a lot. She played with him so much that his first word had been "seven". He was the only thirteen-month-old in the whole wide world who could count to twenty. Zoe was proud of him, but Rafe couldn't help with magnets and he couldn't replace her best friend.

Zoe went upstairs to her room. She wondered what Ava and Rani were doing. Maybe they were watching *Epic* or playing with Ava's dress-up clothes. Instead of the princess dresses everyone else had, Ava had loads of her mum's old real-life dresses to play in. Zoe wondered which one Rani would choose. Surely not the black one with the silver sparkles and feathers. That was Zoe's favourite. And hopefully Rani and Ava weren't talking about magnets; what if Ava decided to work with Rani on the project?

Zoe imagined Ava showing Rani the fairy garden under the big tree behind her house. She pictured Ava's mum serving them both pizza with no meat round Ava's kitchen table, and then maybe those special ice lollies they always had at Ava's house, the kind with sprinkles on.

Could vegetable-arians eat sprinkles?

Zoe was still thinking when it began to get dark. The star stickers above her bed, which were arranged in proper constellations just like in the real night-time sky, began to glow. Zoe's dad had helped her stick them on. He was a scientist who built rockets to go into outer space. He was also very tall, which helped with reaching the ceiling.

"Zoe! Teatime, darling," called Zoe's mum. Zoe could hear her dad and Rafe in the kitchen, and she could smell spaghetti bolognaise.

But even after she'd had her third piece of garlic bread, Zoe was still thinking about Rani.

"Rani doesn't eat meat," Zoe told her mum and dad. "She can't eat cheeseburgers. Isn't that strange?"

"Who is Rani?" asked Zoe's dad.

"Rani is the new girl in Zoe's class," said Zoe's mum. "They moved in across the road from the Hugheses." Hughes was Ava's surname.

"She doesn't eat cheeseburgers!" repeated Zoe.

Rafe must have felt left out. "Seven," he said. "Onetwothreefourfivesixseven."

"That's right," Zoe told him. "No cheeseburgers!" She could always count on Rafe to agree with her.

"How do you know she doesn't eat cheeseburgers?" asked Zoe's dad. "Did she tell you?"

"She's a veterinarian, errr, vegetable-arian," said Zoe. "Because of her religion. Isn't that terrible? No cheeseburgers!"

"You mean she's a vegetarian," said her mum. "Zoe, Grandma and Grandpa Ahlberg don't eat cheeseburgers either, because of their religion. You know that. It's not that terrible."

That was true. Like Zoe, Grandma and Grandpa Ahlberg were Jewish. They kept

something called kosher, which Zoe knew
meant that they didn't eat meat and cheese
together. They also had lots of cutlery at their
house to use for different kinds of food.

"Where has Rani moved from?" Zoe's dad
asked.

"I don't remember," said Zoe. "Somewhere
that starts with L, but isn't London." Zoe had
been so cross after lunch that she hadn't really
listened to Rani going on about where she
came from.

"Onetwothreefourfivesixseveneightnine?"
guessed Rafe, and he laughed alongside
everyone else.

"You need to be kind to Rani," Zoe's mum
said, finally. "Can you imagine how hard it
would be to move schools and to leave all of
your friends behind? Especially as the term has
already started."

Zoe hadn't actually thought about that. She

couldn't imagine leaving Ava. She wondered whom Rani had left behind in that other L place. Some poor girl who was now way more than a few rows away from her Best Friend Forever.

Zoe decided then and there that she would forgive Rani for spoiling the seating plan in Year Three. She would forgive her for wasting two break times and for ruining what should have been a fun magnetic play date. Tomorrow, Zoe would tell Rani all about Grandma and Grandpa Ahlberg, and how they didn't eat cheeseburgers either. Maybe she would also tell her about that fox she had seen on the way to school: the one going to the bus stop. She would be extra, *extra* kind to the new girl.

But it didn't quite turn out that way.

Chapter

The Beginning of Never

Zoe couldn't have been happier to see Ava strolling up the path ahead of her as they went into school that morning. She'd already talked to her mum about having Ava round to work on the magnet project. Zoe's mum was going to ring Ava's mum and it was all going to be sorted out. That would make up for yesterday and everything would be back to normal. And Zoe would be extra, extra, *extra* nice to Rani and maybe even invite her round some time. (But not today, Zoe had decided. Today would just be Ava and Zoe.)

"How was the play date with Rani?" Zoe asked Ava as they pushed open the heavy school door. "Is she nice? What did you do?"

"She's great!" said Ava. "We played Monopoly at mine and then we went across the road to Rani's house and made—"

But Zoe wasn't listening. Ava reached out to stroke Baron Biscuit and Zoe noticed something on her wrist. It was a bracelet made out of brightly coloured threads, with beads woven through it. Zoe had never seen it before.

"What's that?" Zoe interrupted Ava. "Is it new?"

"It's a friendship bracelet," Ava told her excitedly. "Rani and I made them; her mum showed us how. You make the same one as someone else, and that's how you know you are friends. Kind of like our Best Friend necklaces, but you can make it at home."

"So Rani has one too?" asked Zoe carefully.

Her tummy felt a little bit funny.

"Yes, we made them pink and purple and turquoise," said Ava. "And then we put some beads on with the letters of our names, *A*s and *R*s and—"

Zoe had stopped on the stairs. The hustle and bustle of the busy hallway seemed far away. All she could think about was that bracelet.

"But you hardly know Rani!" Zoe said. It came out sounding meaner than she meant it to, but how could you be proper friends after ONE play date?

"I do now," said Ava, moving up the stairs. "And I said we could be her friends. Did you know that Rani is allowed to try on her mum's make-up? And she has a canopy on her bed, just like a princess, and also loads of trophies in her room. She was the fastest runner at her old school—"

They'd reached the Year Three classroom and suddenly there was Lottie, wanting to know all about Rani coming to Ava's house, and then all about Ava going across the road to Rani's house. What did Rani like to play, and what was Ava's new bracelet, and how did you make it, and what were Rani's loads of brothers like, and what colour was her new room?

Rani, Rani, Rani. Zoe was sick of Rani. All thoughts of Grandma and Grandpa Ahlberg and the fox and Rani's long-lost best friend in the other L city flew out of Zoe's mind. Zoe didn't feel sorry for poor old Rani any more. Rani was a best-friend stealer.

As they were waiting for the register, Zoe could see Rani's friendship bracelet. It wasn't a *proper* bracelet, like one from a shop, and it certainly didn't have a magic spell on it. At least, Zoe hoped it didn't.

Zoe wanted to tell Rani that her bracelet didn't mean *best* friends, only *regular* friends. But it was pink and purple and turquoise with *A*s and *R*s all over it and it looked just like Ava's, which Zoe did not like. Not one tiny little bit.

Zoe stared at Rani's bracelet whilst Miss Moody called out their names. She stared at Rani's bracelet instead of copying out their new spelling list. She stared at it when they were meant to be practising their six times tables, and when they took turns reading aloud.

Zoe did not, however, stare at Rani's bracelet when the time came to queue up to go outside for morning break. Miss Moody had barely finished saying "Girls, line up, please" when Zoe tore her eyes from Rani's arm, leapt from her seat, bounded over Lottie, who was bent over tying her shoe, and landed next to Ava's desk. The best friends joined the queue together, and Rani the friend-stealer was left behind.

"It's called Go, Go, Grannies: Gotcha!" said Ava. "Right, Rani?"

Ava was standing with Zoe, Lottie, Isabel and Rani on the playground. She was describing a game that Rani had told her about.

"But we don't have grannies in Mummies and Babies," Lottie told Rani.

"We could," suggested Isabel. "We could have a trip to a granny's house, that would be good."

"You aren't LISTENING," Ava said impatiently. "It isn't grannies in Mummies and Babies. Go, Go, Grannies: Gotcha is its OWN

game. Rani used to play it at her old school."

"You mean, you don't want to play Mummies and Babies?" Lottie asked Ava. "But that's what we always do!"

"We could try something different," said Isabel. "I'm getting a tiny bit tired of Mummies and Babies."

Zoe couldn't believe it. They hadn't played yesterday, and now Ava and Rani, and even Isabel, were ruining Mummies and Babies today too!

"Go, Go, Grannies: Gotcha is sort of like the game It," Ava explained, "except you have to move really, really slowly, like an old granny. Whoever is 'it' says, 'Go, go, grannies,' and everyone has to run away but you have to go in slow motion, right, Rani?" Rani nodded.

"It is very funny," Rani said, "because everyone is reeaaallllyyyy slow but trying to rush too, so you don't get caught! We played it every day at my old school." Rani didn't sound shy and sad any more, Zoe noticed. She sounded like a bossy pants.

"Go, Go, Granny Whatsit is just It," said Zoe, "And playing It is boring. Playing It slowly is even more boring than boring."

"Stop being rude!" Ava told Zoe. "Go, Go, Grannies: Gotcha is not more boring than boring, it's more fun than fun! Isn't it, Rani?"

Zoe knew that Ava could not possibly have known how fun Go, Go, Grannies: Gotcha was because Ava had never played it. Ava had never even *heard* of Go, Go, Grannies: Gotcha until silly old Rani had to move from her silly old school and ruin their break times.

Someone had to be in charge. "We are going to play Mummies and Babies like we always do!" said Zoe. "Rani, if you want to play, you can be the granny."

Lottie nodded in agreement. But Ava wouldn't listen.

"You are not the boss of Rani," said Ava. "Or me either. We want to play Go, Go, Grannies: Gotcha! If you just try it, you will like it! Me and Rani love it!" Ava's voice sounded shoutier with every word. "Besides," she said, "Mummies and Babies is for babies."

There was a gasp all round. Zoe stood there facing Rani and Ava. She looked at them in their matching bracelets, going on and on about grannies as slow as turtles.

Zoe glared at Rani. Rani was definitely, one hundred per cent trying to steal her best friend. But even worse was that Ava was letting herself be stolen!

"Then you and Rani play stupid Go, Go, Grannies on your own," said Zoe to Ava at last. "Because you are not my best friend any more!"

Everything went very quiet. Isabel's jaw fell open. Lottie dropped her notebook. Rani looked

surprised, and then as if she was about to cry. All around Zoe and Ava, the Crabtree girls paused to hear what would happen next. It is not every day at Crabtree School that the bestest of best friends suddenly aren't. The air felt heavy with some sort of dark magic, and Zoe thought of the friendship spell, which definitely wasn't working properly.

"We're not best friends because I won't do what you say?" said Ava. "That's not fair! We're best friends FOREVER."

"No," cried Zoe. "We are best friends for

NEVER!" She hadn't meant to scream, but that's how it came out.

Then the bell went.

Chapter

A Not-Friend Is Far Worse
than an Enemy

That strange feeling in the air lasted for the rest of the day. Suddenly Zoe was VERY important. Everyone in Year Three was watching her and Ava, and not because they had won a race on Sports Day.

ARE YOU FRIENDS WITH AVA ANY MORE? read a note passed to Zoe during their French lesson. Zoe recognized Lottie's handwriting.

Zoe ticked the box for NOT FRIENDS.

That afternoon in the library, Zoe sat as far away from Ava and Rani as she possibly could, with Isabel and Lottie sitting on either side of

ARE YOU...
(TICK ONE)
BEST FRIENDS
REGULAR FRIENDS
NOT FRIENDS
ENEMIES

her. Lottie's purple notebook was open on the table. She was trying to hide it underneath her reading book, but Zoe could see that Lottie had been hard at work on her CHART OF FRIENDSHIP.

"Are you and Ava really not going to be best friends ever again?" Isabel wanted to know.

"Yes, really," said Zoe. "Ava is bossy and mean and Go, Go, Granny Whatsit is the dumbest game I've ever heard of."

"Lottie and I argue sometimes," said Isabel. "Remember, Lottie, when I wanted to see the extra secret special bit of your notebook, and you said no, and I said—"

"Yes, I remember!" Lottie interrupted. "But some things are PRIVATE."

"Shush! Quiet, girls!" said Mrs Shush, peering at them over the top of her own book.

Zoe didn't even *know* that Lottie had an extra secret special bit of her notebook, but

she hardly cared just then. "This is different," Zoe whispered to Isabel. "This is forever."

Then Zoe looked up and noticed that Ava and Rani were watching them. What were they whispering? Something mean about Zoe, probably. Zoe stuck her tongue out at Ava.

Ava's eyes went wide. Then they went very narrow and she looked ... *mean*. Zoe had never seen Ava look like that before, not even when they had argued over who got the lolly with more sprinkles or who got to wear which dress-up dress. Mean-looking Ava whispered to Rani some more. Rani whispered back. After a minute, Ava put her hand up. Mrs Shush went over to her and they had a chat. Then the librarian made her way towards Zoe.

Zoe couldn't believe it. Her best friend forever and ever and happily ever after and as long as we both shall live *had told on her*.

Ava was a tattle-tale, a snitch and a meanie.

And it was all Rani's fault. Or at least it started off as Rani's fault, but now it was Ava's too. Zoe had no idea that her ex-best friend could be so horrible.

When Mrs Shush turned her back, Zoe stuck her tongue out again. In fact she did it twice; once at Ava, and once at Rani.

The second magnetic play date was over before it began.

"I wouldn't play with you," Zoe told Ava, "if you were the last girl in the world. You're a tattle-tale!"

They were stood round the Crabtree School gates waiting for their mums or dads to come and collect them. The Year Three class had made a circle around Zoe and Ava. Rani was next to Ava, with Lady Lovelypaws at her feet. Why did even the school *cat* have to like Rani so much, Zoe wondered.

At first Zoe tried to just ignore Ava and Rani, like she had all afternoon after the library incident. But then Zoe decided Ava should probably know what a horrible person she was.

"I *didn't* tell on you," said Ava. "I just told Mrs Shush that you were hurting Rani's and my feelings." Ava put her arm around Rani, just to show what good friends they were.

"THAT IS THE EXACT SAME THING AS TELLING ON ME!!!!" said Zoe, who found that she was screaming again. It made her angry that Ava's and Rani's feelings were now the same feelings. How did that happen?

"Girls, what is going on?" asked Miss Moody. At first there was silence. Neither Zoe nor Ava knew quite what to say. They just looked down at their shoes.

"Zoe and Ava aren't friends any more," Lottie told Miss Moody helpfully. She opened her notebook. "Zoe says Ava is a tattle-tale and a meanie. Ava says Zoe is bossy and also a baby. Ava says Zoe is only her regular friend, and Zoe says Ava is not her friend."

Somewhere halfway through Lottie's report, Zoe began to cry. So did Ava.

Through her tears, Zoe could see Lottie's friendship chart. Ava and Rani were next to each other on the page. Zoe's name had been crossed out and rewritten; now it floated out in white space on the paper, alone. Without a best friend. Without a magnet partner.

Somehow that last bit made Zoe maddest of all. Miss Moody tried to calm them all down, but there was no going back.

"You can't be best friends with a BABY," Zoe shrieked at Ava. "So I don't need this any more!" She pulled off her half-heart necklace and held it high over her head.

"YOU don't want to be best friends with a TATTLE-TALE," shouted Ava. She tore her own necklace from her neck. "Anyway, YOU broke the spell when you said that you wouldn't be friends with me!"

"No, YOU broke the spell when you made best friends with Rani," screamed Zoe.

Everyone stood perfectly still and silent, watching and waiting. Even Miss Moody couldn't think of anything to say.

"I HATE YOU!" shouted Ava to Zoe and Zoe to Ava. At exactly the same time, they both tossed their necklaces high into the air. Together the half-hearts soared over the top of Crabtree School and disappeared.

There was a crack of lightning and a boom of thunder, and it began to pour with rain.

Even the sky was crying.

Chapter

8

Things Really Begin to Wobble

The next morning, Zoe spent a lot of time waiting next to Baron Biscuit. She pretended to tie her shoes, even though they were Velcro and didn't have laces. She polished the Baron's paws with a tissue from her pocket. She checked in her bag for her spelling homework three times.

Zoe wasn't waiting for Ava, exactly, but she *happened* to be standing there when Ava came in. Zoe also *happened* to have her hand up on Baron Biscuit's back at precisely the right time to show Ava her new bracelet.

"What's that?" asked Ava, who for a minute

seemed to forget they were in a fight. She sounded just like the old Ava. "That's an amazing bracelet."

It was. Yesterday during the big rainstorm, Zoe and her family had got a lift home from school with Isabel's mum. Then Isabel and her mum had popped in for a cup of tea and to play, and it was then Isabel and Zoe had decided to make the best friendship bracelets the world had ever seen.

Isabel was brilliant at crafts, and these Extra Special Friendship Bracelets were even better than Isabel's conker people and her sparkly Christmas snowflakes combined. Standing there in the shadow of Lady Constance Hawthorne's statue, Zoe watched Ava gazing at her wrist in admiration.

The main bit of Zoe's Extra Special Friendship Bracelet — and Isabel's too, for they were exactly the same — was a fat ribbon that had been dipped in glue and coated with purple glitter. Winding round that ribbon in a brightly coloured chain were small pink and green elastic bands. Then, with careful use of more glue and safety pins, Isabel had attached all sorts of buttons and charms, pearls and diamonds and even a few sweeties to each of their bracelets. Zoe's wrist looked glorious resting there on Baron Biscuit's back.

"Isabel and I made them," said Zoe. "It's an Extra Special Friendship Bracelet."

Ava made that mean face again. "You're just copying me and Rani," she said. "Now move your hand so I can stroke Baron Biscuit."

Zoe left her hand exactly where it was. "It's not copying if ours are better!" she said. "You are such a meanie."

"You're the one being mean," hissed Ava. "Now, MOVE OUT OF THE WAY."

Ava reached out to stroke Baron Biscuit.

Accidentally, but really probably on purpose, Ava's hand pushed Zoe's hand out of the way. So now Zoe's best friend for never was *pushing* her. Ava was a meanie *and* a bully! Even though they were much too grown-up for this, Zoe pushed back a little bit. After a few more shoves from either side, Baron Biscuit began to wobble.

No one noticed. Zoe was busy glaring at Ava and Ava was busy glaring at Zoe, so the first either of them knew about Baron Biscuit's dangerous situation was the great *clunk*! as he crashed to the floor.

There was a moment of silence and then panic filled the halls. Baron Biscuit was not at his post to guard Crabtree School! They would all have bad luck forever! Zoe was about to tell Ava about how this was all her fault, but then Mrs Peabody rushed in and scooped the Baron up in her arms. Baron Biscuit's left hind

leg had broken off, and one of his ears had crumbled away. A crowd gathered and after a bit, Nurse Forehead appeared with some plasters and a lolly.

"Will Baron Biscuit be all right, Nurse Forehead?" asked Zoe. She was on her hands and knees collecting all the tiny bits of dust from Baron Biscuit's shattered ear. She noticed that Ava kept looking round to see if anyone had seen the accident. If they had, they'd know it was all Zoe and Ava's fault. It didn't help that Baron Biscuit was sparkling with purple glitter, which had clearly come from Zoe's wrist.

Baron Biscuit's injury proved much too severe for a plaster and an emergency lolly. Colonel Crunch was going to have to get out the superglue. It was all very serious, and no one looked more upset about the whole thing than Ava and Zoe.

Lottie appeared from nowhere, notebook in

hand. Straight away, she saw that Ava and Zoe both looked EXTREMELY guilty. Lottie stared at them through her glasses. She reached out to stroke Baron Biscuit and made a note of the purple glitter that came off on her fingers. Ava and Zoe both had the same purple glitter on their hands which, of course, Lottie also noticed.

"Did you make that bracelet together?" Lottie asked Ava and Zoe. Ava and Zoe shook their heads. "Then why are you both so sparkly?" Colonel Crunch was watching Ava and Zoe closely. He thought they looked guilty too.

"Colonel Crunch," Lottie went on, "did you know that Ava and Zoe aren't friends any more? Zoe says that Ava is a meanie, and—"

"Mind your own business, Lottie!" shrieked Ava, and for the first time in two days, Zoe agreed with her. Lottie glared at both of them as Mrs Peabody shooed everyone to their classrooms.

That morning in Year Three things went from

bad to worse. They were meant to be working on the magnet projects whilst Miss Moody marked some handwriting homework, but no one was discussing the North Pole.

"You don't have to get mad at ME because YOU broke Baron Biscuit," Lottie said to Zoe. "I'm just doing my job investigating."

"It's not your *job*, Lottie," said Zoe crossly. "You're not a real spy. You're a child. Real spies are grown-ups." But Zoe had to admit that, even though she was a child, Lottie had come dangerously close to solving the Case of the Broken Biscuit.

"Ava is right," Lottie told Zoe. "*You* are the meanie. That's why you don't have a best friend."

"I do have a best friend," insisted Zoe. "Look, see? Isabel and I made Extra Special Friendship Bracelets. We're best friends now, too."

"Isabel is MY best friend," said Lottie. She stared at Zoe's bracelet in a way that made Zoe remember watching Rani's wrist the day before.

Zoe knew she shouldn't have said what came out of her mouth next, but she did: "We were going to make you a bracelet, but then Isabel didn't want to."

Lottie's big brown eyes filled with hurt, but instead of crying, she reached for her notebook and scrawled a note to Isabel:

TRUE OR FALSE: I DID NOT WANT TO MAKE AN EXTRA SPECIAL BRACELET FOR LOTTIE TOO.

Chapter

9

Never Can Be Quite Contagious

It turned out to be true; Isabel hadn't wanted to make an Extra Special Friendship Bracelet for Lottie. When Zoe had suggested it, Isabel said no, they could keep these Extra Special Friendship Bracelets just for the two of them. This was really because Isabel wanted to have something private that didn't include Lottie, just like the Extra Special Top Secret bit of Lottie's notebook didn't include Isabel.

"But that's silly," said Lottie, when Isabel explained. "A spy has to have some things that are secrets from EVERYBODY. Even her best friend."

They were in the lunch room with the rest of their class. Isabel and Zoe were sitting next to each other, and Lottie was across from them, with Rani and Ava next to her.

Zoe was cross because Ava had made her break Baron Biscuit, and because she was lonely without a proper best friend.

Ava was cross because Zoe had made *her* break Baron Biscuit.

Lottie was cross because Isabel had left her out on purpose.

Isabel was cross because Lottie cared more about spying than she did about being best friends.

Rani was just tired of all this crossness. She was happy to have found Ava. She was also glad that she had rescued Ava from the meanest best friend in the world. All Rani had seen from Zoe was bossiness and shouting, and now it seemed like Zoe was making everyone else cross too.

"*Real* best friends are not supposed to have secrets," Isabel was saying.

"Yes," said Zoe, loudly enough so Ava could hear her. "*Real* best friends tell each other everything. They don't make stupid bracelets with other people."

This is where things got all muddled up: Zoe was talking about *Ava's* bracelet that she'd made with Rani. But Isabel thought that Zoe was saying that the bracelets Zoe and Isabel had just made were stupid too. The stupid bracelets were confusing everybody.

"What are you talking about, Zoe?" screeched both Isabel and Ava at the same time. Then Lottie and Ava and Zoe and Isabel all started shouting at once. No one was listening to anyone else.

"What are you on about?" yelled a girl from another table. "Stop arguing, or we won't get any golden tickets for being good!"

"Mind your own business!" cried some of Year Three.

And then suddenly everyone in the lunch room was shouting at everyone else, and the crossness that before had been a little circle just around Zoe and her friends spread like a sickness. The noise was deafening. Lady Lovelypaws ran from underneath Rani's chair and jumped into the big bin in the corner.

Zoe couldn't stand it. This whole thing was really all Ava's fault. Ava was the one who should have stuck by her best friend forever, and only Ava could make up for it by saying sorry. Zoe tried to tell Ava this, but Ava was shouting something at her and not listening. Zoe yelled louder and louder, but everyone else did too. It was no use. She had to find another way to get Ava to listen. Zoe stood up from her chair, but loads of other girls were standing up too, and shouting.

Zoe looked down at her plate, with its bits of leftover fish fingers and a few stray peas. She looked at her empty cup of water and her crumpled-up napkin. Then her eyes came to rest on her untouched bowl of Mrs Crunch's famous apple crumble.

Then a person who was stood at Zoe's place, a person who looked just like Zoe but who just *couldn't possibly have actually been Zoe*, reached down, picked up a gooey, slightly warm handful of apple crumble and threw it in Ava's face.

Ava gasped as crumble went *splat!* between her eyes. The rest of Year Three gasped as the crumble dribbled down Ava's cheeks. The entire room gasped when the crumble fell from Ava's face into her lap. And from the bin, Lady Lovelypaws gasped when the crumble finally went *plop!* on to the floor.

"You … you … you … horrible…" Ava

was so shocked by the crumble attack that she couldn't even speak. She grabbed the spoon from her own apple crumble, scooped out a huge helping and, using her spoon as a catapult, she flung the crumble across the table at Zoe.

Splat! Ava's crumble hit Zoe right on the nose. But she was ready for it.

"How about some cream with your crumble?" shouted Zoe. She took a huge pitcher of cream and sloshed it across the table at Ava. Except

that she missed Ava, and the cream hit Lottie.

"Hey!" said Lottie. And then *splat!* went a handful of Lottie's apple crumble in Zoe's ear.

Before long there was an all-out apple crumble war going on, and the grown-ups in the room couldn't do anything about it.

"Take that!!" shouted Year Two as all at once they fired their puddings on Year Three.

"That's for stealing my crayon yesterday!" said one Reception girl to another as she dumped crumble on her head.

Splat! Plop! Slop! went the crumble and the cream. When the bowls and pitchers were empty, the girls scooped up crumble from the tables and the floor, and had another go.

Suddenly the lunch room door opened. Mrs Peabody had expected to find tidy tables of girls quietly enjoying their delicious lunches. Instead, she saw a disaster. Crumble covered everyone in the room, the tables and the floor. Crumble was splattered across the windows and crumble dripped from the ceiling. As the headmistress stood staring, a mushy apple soared through the air and landed right on her shoes.

Mrs Peabody fainted.

Chapter

Crumble and Punishment

"WHO STARTED THIS?" thundered Colonel Crunch.

Colonel Crunch was rarely ever cross, and this was certainly the first time Zoe had ever heard him shout. But a huge batch of his wife's apple crumble completely gone to waste was more than the Colonel could take.

"Who started this?" he repeated, and it didn't take long for the entire room to point the finger at Year Three. Colonel Crunch came and stood beside their table. He looked down at Ava and Zoe and Lottie and Isabel. The Colonel had a feeling that these four were somehow involved in all this mess.

"Lottie?" he said. Lottie could always be counted on to know the facts.

But Lottie said nothing. Spies are good at keeping secrets, when they want to.

"Isabel?" tried Colonel Crunch, staring down at her. Isabel was the best-behaved girl in the entire school. Surely she wouldn't approve of this behaviour.

But Isabel said nothing. Just because you know how to behave properly doesn't mean you should tell on everyone else.

"Ava?" Colonel Crunch was getting desperate.

Zoe could hardly breathe. Their whole table could hardly breathe. Surely Ava would tell on her best friend for never, her not-friend, her ex-magnetic partner?

Ava said nothing. Because, when it really came down to it, this was much too big of a thing to tell on someone for. Especially when you might get in trouble too.

Ava shook her head. As she did, a blob of apple crumble fell from her hair on to her lap.

Colonel Crunch turned to Zoe. Her stomach felt like it had wasps in it, and her arms and legs were like jelly. She couldn't lie to Colonel Crunch.

"It was me!" Zoe said as she burst into tears. "I did it! I crumbled Ava! But only because she was mean to me."

Zoe cried and cried. She cried for the mess, for the trouble she was going to be in, and most of all, Zoe cried for her best friend forever, who wasn't any more.

"Attention!" said Colonel Crunch to the rest of the room. "You are all dismissed! Out you go to the playground. Mrs Crunch will rinse you off with the hose."

Mrs Crunch looked delighted at the prospect

of squirting the dozens and dozens of sticky girls who had wasted her precious crumble with a bit of cold water. Revenge is sweet.

"Zoe, you stay here. You too, Ava. You two have a job to do."

Colonel Crunch was not interested in knowing the details of Ava and Zoe's battle. He didn't want to hear all about their falling out, or what they'd said to each other or whose fault it was. He simply handed them each a mop, a bucket and a sponge. Then he left, closing the lunch room door behind him.

Zoe and Ava were alone with Lady Lovelypaws, who was very kindly helping to clean up the cream.

The two girls mopped in silence on opposite sides of the room. At first, they made a big show of ignoring each other. Then Zoe began thinking about how this was probably

not going to be their only punishment. Mrs Peabody might ring their parents, once she was finished fainting. Maybe Ava's mummy and Zoe's mummy would have to come to school early to get them. Then the mummies would see the crumble-covered lunch room and they'd both faint too. Zoe couldn't help smiling a little, in spite of how sad she was. It was a shame that she and Ava weren't ever speaking to each other again. Ava would have liked to imagine a huge pile of shocked, fainting grown-ups next to the dining-room door.

The silence went on and on.

Who would say something first? Not Zoe, that was for sure. Zoe was never, ever, ever going to speak to Ava again. No matter what happened. Never.

But that didn't mean that she couldn't try to get *Ava* talking. Just to see what would happen, Zoe stuck her tongue out at Ava.

It worked. Ava gasped. Lady Lovelypaws looked up from a huge puddle of cream. Then, at last, Ava broke the silence.

"Why are you being so mean?" cried Ava. "You really are the meanest girl in the whole world!"

"No. YOU are," said Zoe. "You are supposed to be my best friend. You chose Rani instead and you broke the spell and hurt my feelings. You ruined everything."

"YOU are the one who said we weren't best friends any more!" said Ava. "YOU broke the spell and hurt MY feelings."

The room seemed to darken at the mention of the spell. Zoe thought sadly about their lost necklaces. Maybe magic didn't really exist after all.

There was a loud hiccup from their feet. Lady Lovelypaws had drunk too much cream.

Zoe had forgotten that she had been the first

to say that Ava wasn't her best friend. It did sound mean, now that she thought about it.

Suddenly, Ava slipped on a particularly gooey bit of apple. She went sliding under the Year Three table.

To prove to Ava that she wasn't the meanest girl in the world, Zoe very, *very* kindly reached down to help Ava to her feet. But then Zoe slipped too, and ended up under the table next to Ava. They both laughed for a second before they remembered not to. They sat under the table together in not-so-terrible silence.

"Remember in Reception," said Zoe at last, "when you fell out of your chair and your jacket potato fell on your head?" As soon as she said it, she worried that Ava might think it was mean to remind her about falling down.

"Yes," said Ava. "And you sat down next to me and we had lunch on the floor. Then we were best friends."

Zoe wondered if they were still best friends.

"You said you hated me," said Zoe finally. "Yesterday."

"So did you. And you ticked 'Not Friends' on Lottie's note," replied Ava.

"I'm sorry I ticked that box," said Zoe. She meant it. "I was mad at you because you chose Rani as your best friend instead of me."

Now that she wasn't *quite* as angry as she had been, Zoe had a very scary question that she needed to ask Ava.

"Is Rani your best friend?" asked Zoe.

"No," said Ava, and Zoe's heart skipped a beat. "But I really like her. You would too, if you gave her a chance. You should have been nicer to her."

Zoe thought about Rani ruining break time and stealing her best friend. She thought about how much she wanted things to go back to the way they had been before Rani had come to Crabtree School. But she realized that this wasn't really about Rani. What Zoe really wanted to know was whether she and Ava were still best friends, whether they could forgive each other. But that was hard to talk about.

"OK," was all Zoe said. "If you like Rani, I will be nice to her."

"Good," said Ava.

"But only because you are my best friend," Zoe added quickly. She held her breath.

Ava nodded in agreement.

After that, there was no more explaining, or saying sorry, or pointing out whose fault it was. Sometimes best friends don't need words. Besides, the crumble was going from gooey to sticky, and poor Lady Lovelypaws had drunk so much cream that she was turning green.

The two friends got back to the job at hand. Working side-by-side, they wiped and mopped and scrubbed. When they were finished, the lunch room shone.

It was as if the whole terrible thing had never happened. Almost.

It was still break time when Colonel Crunch dismissed Ava and Zoe into the playground.

Isabel, Lottie and Rani were in the corner near the slide with a few other Year Three girls. They were playing It, but they were all moving so slowly that it was hard to tell if they were really moving at all. They looked really, really silly. And they were all laughing. "Go, Go, Granny: Gotcha!" shouted Lottie as she tagged Rani in slow motion.

"Do you want to play?" Ava asked Zoe timidly.

"Yes," said Zoe. "But could we play Mummies and Babies tomorrow?"

"Sure," said Ava. "If you want to."

They took off across the playground, as

slowly as they possibly could. Rani looked surprised when she saw Zoe coming, and a little scared, but they soon got lost in the game. Remembering to be as slow as a turtle when you are trying to run away from someone takes a lot of brain power. There was no time to worry about anything else.

In the end, Go, Go, Grannies: Gotcha *did* turn out to be more fun than fun. Especially when Rani suggested that they combine it with Mummies and Babies. Now it was way more than just a slow version of It. In their new game, the baby had to crawl, the mummies and daddies could run normally, the lifeguard had to pretend to swim and of course the granny had to be slow. And every once in a while, Zoe would transform into a fox, like the one she'd seen on his way to the bus stop. If the fox was chasing you, you could run as fast as you wanted, even if you were a granny. When the fox appeared, cries of "Gotcha!" could be heard for miles around.

Chapter

Friendship All Around

Zoe was more nervous than nervous. In just a minute, she was going to have to stand up and give a talk in front of all of the twenty-one girls in her class, plus Miss Moody, plus Mrs Peabody, who had come to watch the Year Three magnet presentations. That made twenty-three people, and twenty-three people made Zoe quite scared, she realized. She looked at Rani in front of her, and thought about how scary it must have been to stand up in front of twenty-three strangers on her first day. (Zoe was glad that they weren't strangers any more.

She'd even given Rani her pink Monday pencil, to make up for being unkind. Rani had given her a sparkly purple one in return.)

Ava's magnet presentation was about her plan to use a giant magnet to trap Father Christmas by his metal belt when he came down the chimney. (Ava had refused to believe that this project wasn't about Christmas.) Zoe, Isabel, Lottie and Rani had laughed so hard they cried.

Lottie and Isabel had got permission to bring in Lottie's dog, Pip, to demonstrate his magnetic collar and lead, and Rani had brought in earrings that looked like they were for pierced ears but were really magnets. Zoe wasn't allowed to have her ears pierced, so Rani's project was just about the best thing she had ever seen.

Now it was Zoe's turn.

"My project is about magnets and friendship," began Zoe nervously. The class listened carefully. They all knew what a tough thing friendship could be to explain.

"We all have friends," said Zoe. "Sometimes we have best friends. Sometimes we don't and sometimes friends change and that can be hard." She looked at Ava and smiled. Ava smiled back.

"Sometimes best friends have things like special bracelets and necklaces," Zoe went on. "And sometimes those things can hurt your feelings or make you feel left out. I know this because it happened to me."

Zoe could feel all forty-six of the eyes in the classroom watching her closely. She reached into a bag that was near her feet and took out a perfectly ordinary beaded bracelet. She held it up in front of all those eyes.

"I thought magnets might be able to help us all not feel left out," explained Zoe. "This is a normal bracelet. There is no spell on it, and no glitter and no sweeties, but it is very special. On each end, there is a magnet. When you bring the magnets together, they attract and that holds the bracelet on you."

Zoe demonstrated this on her own wrist. Everyone clapped.

"Well done, Zoe," said Miss Moody. "Yes, magnets can be used in jewellery-making, like Rani's earrings and your bracelet—"

"Wait, Miss Moody," said Zoe, "there's more." She reached into her bag and took out another bracelet, the same as the first.

"Sometimes you are best on your own, like this." Zoe held up her wrist with the first bracelet on it. "But sometimes you can put your bracelet together with someone else's, and make something different, like this." Zoe took off the bracelet she was wearing. She used the magnets on either end to connect it to the second bracelet, so it made a longer bracelet, which was actually long enough to be a necklace.

Zoe put the necklace on Isabel. Then she reached into her bag and took out twenty more beaded bracelets. She passed them around the class. There was one for everyone.

"I made these for us because we are *all* friends," said Zoe. "And I thought we could take turns putting them together and making all kinds of fun jewellery. Crowns and bracelets and anklets... But everyone has one of their

own to remind them that they are a part of this class and that they always have friends, even when things go wrong with best friends."

Miss Moody looked very proud. Mrs Peabody beamed from the back row. Colonel Crunch, who had been watching from the doorway, nodded approvingly. Everyone in Year Three clapped and cheered.

Zoe's magnet project was a cracking success, and she'd done it all on her own.

Later that day, after he'd glued Baron Biscuit back at his post in the hallway, Colonel Crunch spied something way up on the roof of the Crabtree School tree house. Something was caught on the weathervane. Something shiny. Once he'd fetched his binoculars, Colonel Crunch could see that it was a necklace hanging there. After he'd dragged out his gigantic ladder, the Colonel discovered that what he'd actually found were *two* necklaces – two halves of the same heart. Together they spelled out BEST FRIENDS.

Colonel Crunch had no idea how the necklaces had got way up there, though he had a feeling that they belonged to Ava and Zoe. The friends were delighted to have them back. It was quite something to think that the spell had been hanging over their heads this whole time, working its magic. True friendship spells are like that: sometimes you think they've been broken forever, and the friendship is over. Usually, though, the magic is still out there, just waiting to be rediscovered some day.

Zoe and Ava wore the necklaces all the time. Zoe also wore the Extra Special Friendship Bracelet she had made with Isabel, and Ava and Rani wore their threaded bracelets, the ones with the *A*s and the *R*s. Isabel and Lottie decorated safety pins to wear on the straps of their shoes. And of course, every girl in Year Three had the bracelet that Zoe had made for her magnet project. On any given day there were long necklaces and glittery bracelets and sparkly pins and twinkling tiaras – it made Zoe smile to count them.

From that day onwards, for forever and ever and happily ever after, Crabtree School shone with the sparkle of friendship, and there was magic in all of it.

Turn the page
for lots more
Crabtree School
fun!

ALL ABOUT ME

MY FULL NAME: Zoe Eloise Ahlberg

WHERE I LIVE: 1 Apple Street

WHAT MY ROOM LOOKS LIKE: My room is white and pink and purple and red and green and blue. It has one bed, one desk and one chair. It has twenty-two toys in it. It also has stars on the ceiling that glow in the dark. The stars make constellations just like in the real sky.

WHO IS IN MY FAMILY: My mum, who is a doctor, my dad, who is a scientist, and my brother, Rafe, who is a baby.

MY PETS: I have zero pets.

MY BEST FRIEND(S): Ava Hughes is my bestest

best friend, and also Lottie and Isabel and Rani. (They are age seven, seven, eight and seven.)

WHAT I LOVE TO DO: I like to make Lego and to dress up with Ava. I also like to go to the movies.

WHAT MAKES ME CROSS: Anything that is not fair makes me VERY cross.

WHAT I AM MOST AFRAID OF: GHOSTS! I do NOT like the ghost stories that Ava tells when we have sleepovers!

WHAT I COLLECT: Watches. I have five!!!!!

MY SECRET HIDING PLACE: I have a treasure chest that is really a puzzle. I built it with my dad. It has a lock and a hinged lid and everything. I keep it under my bed.

Ava, Zoe, Isabel, Lottie and Rani are all friends at the end of the story. Now here's your chance to write all about your friends!

ALL ABOUT MY FRIENDS by

_____

Everyone has special qualities and talents. Can you write down things you really like about your friends? Is your friend helpful and kind, like Isabel, or great at making up games, like Rani? Or maybe your friend is good at pretending, like Ava and Zoe?

MY FRIEND'S NAME IS

_____

And I like my friend because:

_____

_____

_____

MY FRIEND'S NAME IS:

_____

And I like my friend because:

_____

_____

_____

MY FRIEND'S NAME IS:

_____

And I like my friend because:

_____

_____

_____

MY FRIEND'S NAME IS:

_____

And I like my friend because:

_____

_____

_____

WHICH CRABTREE CHARACTER ARE YOU?

1. What's your favourite colour?
a. Blue
b. Purple
c. Pink
d. It changes all the time
e. Hot pink with sparkles

2. Choose a pet:
a. Cat
b. You don't want any pets
c. Rabbit
d. Dog
e. You want a pet so badly that you'd be happy
   with anything

3. What would you like to collect?
a. Snow globes
b. Watches

c. Bits of absolutely anything and everything

d. Spy equipment

e. Nail polish

4. What do you love to do in your spare time?

a. Reading

b. Solving puzzles

c. Arts and crafts

d. Watching movies

e. Sports

5. Choose a Halloween costume:

a. A fairy

b. Cruella de Vil

c. A witch

d. A vampire

e. Disney princess

6. What's the best thing about you?

a. You've got a big imagination

b. You're clever

c. You're really well-behaved

d. You're curious about everything

e. You're very sporty

7. If you're honest, you can be:

a. A bit messy

b. A bit bossy

c. A bit too worried about the rules

d. A bit nosy

e. A bit competitive

8. What makes you cross?

a. People interrupting you

b. Other people's mess

c. When you can't get any time to yourself

d. Secrets you don't know

e. Not being the best at something

RESULTS

Mostly As: You're like Ava!

You're a daydreamer with a big imagination. You love reading and dressing up and playing with your friends. You can be a little bit messy, and sometimes you stop listening to what people are saying because you're so busy making up stories. Most of all, you're easy to get on with and kind to everyone and everything.

Mostly Bs: You're like Zoe!

You love numbers and solving puzzles and you're always the first person to put your hand up in class. You can be a little bossy sometimes and you don't like it when things aren't fair. You're a very loyal friend and you're brilliant at helping people with their problems.

Mostly Cs: You're like Isabel!

You're really creative and you almost never get into trouble because you do everything you can to be good. Your bedroom is always tidy even though you make lots of crafts. Sometimes you'd like to relax and not be such a goody-two-shoes. When you do, you tell great jokes and make everyone laugh.

Mostly Ds: You're like Lottie!

You're a spy in training! You're curious and you notice everything around you – no one can keep secrets when you're about! But you also keep those secrets to yourself because you're very loyal. You love watching movies at the cinema and on TV.

Mostly Es: You're like Rani!

You're really sporty and competitive and would love to win an Olympic medal one day, but

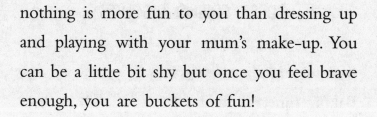

nothing is more fun to you than dressing up and playing with your mum's make-up. You can be a little bit shy but once you feel brave enough, you are buckets of fun!

BEST FRIEND BISCUITS

Making time: 5 minutes

Baking time: 15 minutes

Ingredients: (Makes about 30 biscuits)

250g butter, softened

140g caster sugar

1 egg yolk

2 tsp vanilla extract

300g plain flour

How to make your best friend biscuits:

1. Heat your oven to 180°C/fan 160°C/gas mark 4 and lightly grease a non-stick baking sheet.

2. Mix the butter and the caster sugar in a large bowl with a wooden spoon.

3. To the bowl, add the egg yolk (ask an adult to separate the egg for you!) and vanilla extract and briefly beat the mixture together

4. Sift over the plain flour and stir it all up until the mixture is combined – get your hands in there towards the end and make sure it's all really well mixed!

5. Put some flour on the work surface and roll out your dough so it's about one centimetre thick and cut out your biscuits using a biscuit cutter of your choice. If you want, you can ask an adult to make a line down the middle of the biscuit using a dull knife. That way, when it is baked, you can break it in half easily and share it with your best friend! (Be careful not to make the cut too deep, or one biscuit will become two too early!)

6. Put the biscuits on to your baking tray, but keep them slightly apart because they'll grow in the oven!

7. Ask an adult to put your biscuits in the oven for 12-15 minutes. Take them out when they're golden brown. Carefully put them on a cooling rack until they firm up.

8. Decorate them however you want! You could use icing and sparkles, and if you are baking them with a friend, each of you can do one half of the same biscuit.

9. Once you've finished decorating, break a biscuit in half and share with your best friend, your mummy or your little brother.

CRABTREE SCHOOL

Collect all the Crabtree School books!

Win a family set of scooters!

To celebrate the brilliant Crabtree School series we've got four brand new Micro Scooters® to give away! The lucky winner will also receive a signed set of four Crabtree School books.

Scooting as a family is the perfect way to spend quality time together; you can travel in style and then snuggle down at story time with the Crabtree School gang. Ideal for lots of family fun, you won't want to miss out on this amazing prize!

Visit **www.crabtreeschool.com** to enter the free competition before it closes at midnight on 31st December 2015.

Good luck!

*T&Cs apply – visit **www.crabtreeschool.com** for full details

www.micro-scooters.co.uk